Ryder

ADVENTURES AWAIT AS SOON AS
FLIGHT TAKES PLACE

Skylar

NASHVILLE

ATAPWG

ARDNEK 3d
An imprint of Ardnek 3d LLC

For more information contact
Ardnek3d at www.ardnek3d.com
Written and illustrated by Kendra Hudson
Edited by Brittani Purifie
ISBN 9781735535609

Library of Congress Cataloging-in-Publication Data is available upon request
Printed in the United States of America
10 9 8 7 6 5 4 3 2 1
First Edition

FLYING THROUGH
NASHVILLE

Written and Illustrated by
Kendra Hudson

"GOOD MORNING SKYLAR!"
screams Ryder.
"Today we will be flying through
NASHVILLE, TENNESSEE!"
"May I please sleep for 10 more minutes big brother?" whines Skylar.

"No way! We're ready for takeoff!"

"Do I have to? Just wake me later!"

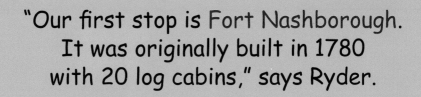

"Our first stop is Fort Nashborough.
It was originally built in 1780
with 20 log cabins," says Ryder.

"Maybe I can hide in cabin 3
and take a nap," says Skylar.

"Not a chance little sister!"
Ryder says jokingly.

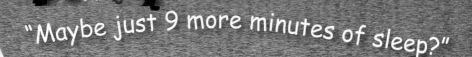

"Maybe just 9 more minutes of sleep?"

"Our next stop is
Bicentennial Capitol Mall," says Ryder.

"Did you say mall? Well, where are
the stores?" questions Skylar.

"This 19-acre state park opened in
1996 to celebrate the 200th
anniversary of the Volunteer State.

It features an amphitheater, tons of cool exhibits, and important history. My favorite is The Court of 3 Stars, surrounded by the 95-bell carillon that plays *The Tennessee Waltz* every hour," says Ryder.

"Oh great, a lullaby to help me sleep!"

"Up next is the Tennessee State Capitol that opened in 1859. Did you know that it's one of the few without a dome?" asks Ryder.

"Thanks for the fun facts," gripes
Skylar. "But ummm... Can I just
sleep a little longer?"

In his best reporter
voice Ryder yells,

"Flying right ahead!"

"Next stop is the Parthenon" says Ryder.

"Part-he-none...What did you say?" questions Skylar.

"It's pronounced *Parthenon*," Ryder says slowly. "Located in Centennial Park, it's the exact size as the original in Athens, Greece."

"Wow, that's interesting," yawns Skylar.

"Maybe just 7 more minutes of sleep!"

"How can you think about sleeping with all those cheering football fans down there?" says Ryder.

Skylar yells over the cheering fans,

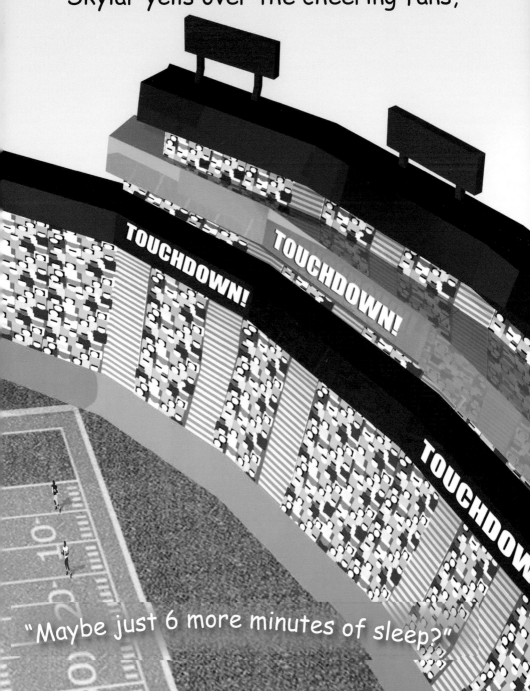

"Maybe just 6 more minutes of sleep?"

"Okay, let's check out Bridgestone Arena. It hosts sporting events, concerts, award ceremonies, and so much more! Most importantly, it's the home of Nashville's hockey team. Back in 2003, someone threw a catfish on the ice, and now it's a Nashville tradition," says Ryder.

"Well, that's weird," Skylar says.

"Just next door, we have the new National Museum of African American Music. The museum has 6 galleries that showcase over 50 genres of music. It has a collection of over 1,400 collectables," says Ryder.
"Also, did you know that Nashville's nickname is

MUSIC CITY!"

PUBLIC MARKET

"Wow, Music City!" sings Skylar.

"You won't need sleep after this sweet treat! Next stop is Goo Goo Shop. This chocolate cluster was the 1st combination candy bar in the world. It was created in 1912," Ryder says.

"WOW, the entire world!" says Skylar.

"This will wake you up for sure.
It's Nashville Zoo at Grassmere!
They have over 2,764 animals,"
says Ryder.

"Wow, look a giraffe!" Skylar says.

"How about a splash of fun?
This is Nashville Shores.
They have over 1 million
gallons of water, and 9 water
slides for loads of summer fun!"
says Ryder. "Not to mention,
they also have
Treetop Adventure Park.
It offers not 1 but 10
huge zip lines, cargo nets, and
so much more."

With great excitement Skylar says, "Wow! I spot a purple slide that looks cool, and the kids look like they're having so much fun!

Water is my absolute favorite!"

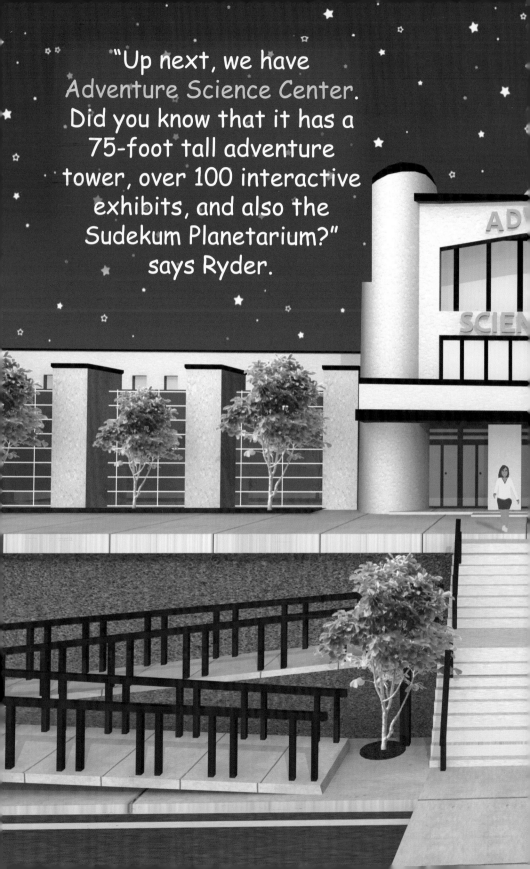

"Up next, we have Adventure Science Center. Did you know that it has a 75-foot tall adventure tower, over 100 interactive exhibits, and also the Sudekum Planetarium?" says Ryder.

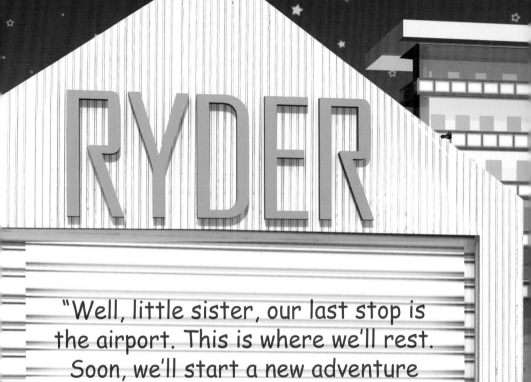

"Well, little sister, our last stop is the airport. This is where we'll rest. Soon, we'll start a new adventure in a new city!" yawns Ryder.

"Today was AWESOME! Nashville gets an A+ in our travel book!" Skylar says with a smile.

RYDER AND SKYLAR'S
TRAVEL BOOK

A+

What city should we visit next?
Cast your vote at www.ardnek3d.com